This book belongs to:

_____

Almondine

Gabriele Zucchelli

Acknowledgements:

Huge thanks to Ian Long, Konrad Welz, Nicky Stockley,
Deborah Murrell, Alba, Nina and Anna Godas
for their invaluable contribution.

BOOKS

Published by GZ Books

Print Book ISBN: 978-1-8383209-0-4

ePub ISBN: 978-1-8383209-1-1

www.almondine.club

Special thanks:

Julia & Montserrat

Contents

Prologue

What's it like to be a mother?
I bet you're not even thinking about that now, dear reader. You're far too young, so why should you? You have friends to play with, school to go to, activities to teach you new things and lots of games to occupy your time.
But this wasn't the case for Alma.
Who'd have thought that an ordinary girl her age would suddenly find herself looking after a baby? And a particularly weird baby, at that.

Chapter 1

A Strange Almond

It all started during her Christmas holiday.

Every winter, Alma and her family spent the school break with her grandparents at their big old country house in Spain.

And now, it was already time to leave. Alma and her mother had just agreed which of her presents were allowed to be taken back to London, and she was lying down on the sofa to play with her new collection of Robo-Doll cards.

Her mother was in the kitchen with Grandma, squeezing some special treats into the family's big suitcase. They were discussing food so loudly that

Alma couldn't quite tell if they were arguing or just having an enjoyable chat.

And all that talk of food was making Alma's tummy rumble.

'Mum, I'm hungry!'

Alma's mother often wondered where she got her endless appetite!

'Can I have some chocolate?'

'You've had too much already.'

Then Grandma had an idea.

'I've got something better than chocolate for you. From our tree. I'll go and get it.'

When she came back, she put a little wicker basket on the table. Nestling on its embroidered lining, Alma found a handful of almonds and an old nutcracker.

Alma would have preferred chocolate, but she thought the nuts might be nice, too.

'You can crack them yourself,' Grandma said.

Alma put the almonds on the table, then, using all her strength, she cracked one open and popped it into her mouth. It tasted delicious.

After a while, Alma had eaten all the almonds except one. It was a particularly stubborn one to open. The palm of her right hand was starting to feel a bit sore, so she changed the nut's position in the nutcracker a few times and kept on squeezing as hard as she could with both hands. Then...
'Aoo!'
Alma heard a tiny squeak.

It seemed to be coming from inside her hands. She thought it must be her imagination.

Once again, she tried to crack the almond.

'Aoo!'

'What is that?!' Alma said to herself.

She dropped the nutcracker and looked under the table. But nothing was there.

'Aoo… aoo…'

More tiny cries came from the nut on the table. Alma carefully picked it up and put it close to her ear. Nothing. She shook it.

'Aaaaa…' the almond cried again.

'Aaaaa!' Alma shouted, too.

She put the almond on the table and stared at it.

'Alma, are you OK? Did you hurt your fingers?' her mother called from the kitchen.

'No… I'm fine,' Alma said.

She cautiously picked up the almond again. It seemed to be trembling slightly.

'This nut is alive!' she whispered to herself.

She clenched it in her fist, grabbed the nutcracker and left the table.

As Alma hurried through the hallway, her father walked in through the front door with Grandad and his dog, Rex, a frisky young spaniel.

'Where are you going with that nutcracker?' asked her father.

'Just playing… I'll bring it back,' she replied, and headed to their guest bedroom.

Rex started to bark loudly at her.

'Stop it, Rex! What's got into you?' Grandad said with a frown. But Rex kept on barking at Alma until Grandad had to reprimand him again. Reluctantly, Rex slunk off to his favourite cushion.

Alma entered their guest room downstairs and closed the door. She was alone. She sat on her parents' bed and opened her fist.
'What kind of almond is this?' she wondered.

Chapter 2

Crack!

Alma turned the almond in her fingers, exploring its every detail. It looked like a perfectly ordinary one, nothing special.

She shook it again. Nothing happened.

Had she imagined those sounds? Because now, the almond was completely quiet.

She waited in the dimly lit room, mustering the courage to try cracking it again.

She gripped it with the nutcracker. At first she pressed gently, then a bit harder. Not a single sound came from it.

C'mon, this is crazy, she thought. *It's just a nut.*

Then she squeezed it really hard, until it finally cracked in half.

But when Alma opened the shell, instead of a tasty almond, she found a tiny baby girl cradled inside. The soft light of the room roused the baby, who stretched her arms and looked around.

Alma quickly closed her hands. Her friends always said she had a vivid imagination, but this was really too much.

'Aoo… aoo…'

The squeaky little cry came again from inside Alma's hands. 'This is real!' she told herself. Alma slowly opened her hands. The little girl was waving her arms and legs around and whimpering in her tiny voice. 'Shhh!' Alma urged her. 'Shhh! Don't cry.'

She gently rocked the girl in her hands to calm her down. Gradually, the baby's crying turned into an irresistible giggle.

'Ueh!… ooah!… guu!… guu!… ga!… ga!…'

This made Alma smile. The baby was fully awake now and becoming excited.

Alma lightly rubbed her belly and the baby seemed to like it and immediately hugged the tip of Alma's finger. At school, Alma had seen photos of baby koalas holding on to their mothers exactly like that. She lifted her finger with the baby firmly

holding on to it, and looked at her more closely.
'You are so adorable.'

'Almaaa!! Get ready, we have to leave soon!' her
mother called from upstairs.

'OK!!!' Alma
shouted back.
The baby
stared wide-
eyed at Alma.
Then she uttered
a loud, plaintive cry.
'Uaaaaaa!!!'
'No, no! It's OK, I'm not
shouting at you. Shhh…
please calm down… shush…'
Alma hummed a made-up lullaby
and gently rocked her hands back
and forth again.
But it didn't seem to work.
'Shhh…' Alma kept on hushing the little
girl. 'What am I going to do with you?'
'Alma!!! The bags are in the car, put your
jacket on!' her mother was calling again.
'Where are you?'
'Mum's coming,' Alma said to the baby. 'Where
am I going to put you?'

She glanced around the room.

An old doll was lying sadly on a small car seat in a corner. Her plastic shoes could work as a cradle, Alma thought.

Alma's mother stormed into the room.

'Check that you haven't forgotten anything! Where have you put your jacket?'

Alma stood up stiffly, holding the doll, and gave her mother a big smile.

'You're not taking that with you now! You haven't looked at it all the time we've been here.'

'Nope! I'm not.'

Alma dropped the doll, now only wearing one shoe, and left the room. Outside, Grandma gave her a warm hug and Alma thanked her for this amazing holiday – she was so looking forward to going home with her secret discovery!

Finally, they were all squeezed inside the little car and ready for their trip to the airport.

'Always late!' Grandad complained from the driving seat.

They left, waving at Grandma until she was out of view. For the whole journey, Alma kept her hand over the pocket of her jacket. In her mind, she was begging the baby:

Please don't cry, please don't cry, please don't cry…

Chapter 3

At the Airport

The baby was suspiciously quiet throughout the whole journey. Was she all right? Alma hoped she wasn't suffocating in her pocket.

Occasionally she sneaked a look inside, and although she could see the shoe, she couldn't see where the baby was.

Alma wanted to hold her with her fingers, but was afraid the baby would start crying again if she was touched.

Mum would probably take the baby away if she found out about her, Alma thought. *Maybe she'd call a hospital, or the police – or the newspapers!*

No, this little baby is mine, and mine only.

Finally they arrived at the airport, Grandad left, and they went to queue at the departures gate.
It was time to walk through security.
Oh no, the security scanners! Alma thought. *I need to take off my jacket now.*
She undressed carefully and gingerly placed her jacket on the tray. All safe.
Or at least it was until her dad slammed his jacket, his shoes, and all the rest of his clutter on to the tray, and then squeezed everything down for good measure.

'Watch out, Dad! Alma shouted. 'Be careful.'
'Is there something fragile in your coat?' her father asked, surprised. 'Take it out, then.'
'No!!! Leave it.'
Alma jumped in front of her dad and guarded the tray until it disappeared into the scanner.

She watched the security lady at the monitor.
'Oh no, she's going to spot her.'
Alma covered her face. The conveyor belt stopped.

That's it, she thought.

But after a few seconds it started moving again.
The baby must have stayed still and gone through
completely unnoticed.

Alma grabbed her coat.

'I need the toilet,' she told her mother.

'OK, let's find one.'

They collected all their belongings and quickly
put their coats back on.

After a short walk, her mum spotted a toilet.

'There you go. I'll come with you.'

'I can go on my own,' Alma declared.

She locked herself in a cubicle. Feeling safe, she
pulled the plastic
shoe from her
pocket and
looked
inside.
And there
was the baby,
cuddled up at
the tip.
'Good, you're
safe,' Alma
whispered.

The baby opened her eyes.

'Ga!'

'Shhh… go back to sleep.'

'Ga! Gaa… fa, fa, ooa, ooa!' the baby babbled as she crawled out of the shoe and on to Alma's hand. She was a bit more energetic now, and her eyes twinkled with excitement and curiosity. Alma couldn't resist.

'Hey, cutie, are you OK?'

'Eeu… ogghey…'

Alma smiled.

'Now get back inside the shoe. Off you go, we have a long trip ahead.'

'Lon… dib… aeh,' the baby copied her.

'That's right. Now get back in.'

Alma delicately pushed her in with her finger.

'Go back to sleep.'

'Gah… baaa… dooo… leee...'

The baby was getting quite chatty.

'Stay in there and hush, now.'

Alma put the shoe back in her pocket, waited till the voice stopped, and left the toilet. Her mother was waiting outside.

'What took you so long? Dad is already queuing. Is everything OK?'

'Yeah,' Alma replied evasively, and hurried

towards the gate.
She could hear muffled sounds
coming from her pocket.
She put her hand
back inside,
hoping to
comfort the
little one, and
noticed that
she'd crawled
out of the shoe
and was tearing
away at a paper
tissue. Alma tried to
grab her.

Her playful shouts seemed louder now. Surely everyone around could hear them?

Alma decided the best solution was to sing over the sound, so nobody would notice.

'Alma, we're nearly at the gate. Come back and keep close to us.'

Alma came nearer, singing.

'You're very chipper this evening,' her father observed.

'Fly me to the moon… and let me shush you… baby shush…'

As Alma sang, the baby fidgeted and tickled her fingers, making Alma pull funny faces. She was very ticklish.

They were nearly at the boarding gate when the baby found her way up Alma's wrist under her sleeve and crawled up to her elbow.

'What spring is like on Jupiter and Maaaaaaa!!!' Alma shrieked, improvising a routine of bizarre street dancing steps.

'Alma, stop being silly!' said her mum.

Alma could feel little hands and feet crawling towards her armpit.

'Is she OK?' asked the hostess at the gate, looking at Alma with concern.

'Yes, she's fine,' Alma's mother reassured her, unconvincingly.

'Cut it out, Alma! This is no time to rehearse your dance steps!' her father reproached her.

The miniature baby had climbed up to her chest, and

Alma just couldn't keep still. 'She's just a bit tired. It's been a long journey.'

By now, Alma's singing had turned into one long, unstoppable giggle.

'Have a good flight,' said the hostess, handing back their passports.

Alma couldn't control herself. The baby had crawled around her tummy and was now slowly creeping up her back.

They entered the aeroplane.

'26 A B C. Over there.'

As they squeezed past the other passengers to get their seats, Alma could feel the baby crawling up her neck.

'Hahahaaa!' she couldn't hold back her laughter.

Other passengers noticed Alma's weird behaviour. Some smiled, others turned away.

'Alma, will you just stop?' her mother insisted, as her father stowed their bags in the overhead locker. 'And take off your coat.'

'No… ooaaa…' Alma giggled.

Her mother, who was already stressed out by the journey, briskly pulled off Alma's coat.

'I need to keep it on!' Alma shouted.

But her mother handed the coat to her father, who squeezed it into the overhead locker.

Sitting down in a window seat, Alma felt around her body. Where had the baby gone?

Chapter 4

On the Aeroplane

It was time to fasten the seat belts.

Alma was panicking and searching all over her body. Had she squashed the baby?

'What are you looking for?' her mother asked.

'Nothing.'

'Come on. What have you lost?'

'Nothing,' Alma repeated. 'Can I have my coat back, please?'

'Not now. Fasten your seat belt,' her mother said, fanning herself with her ticket.

The little girl had to be inside her coat. Just a few minutes to wait, and she could make sure.

The plane took off as the sun was setting. Alma
eagerly waited for the 'ding' sound, signalling she
could take off her seat belt.
It seemed an eternity. And then: 'ding!'
'Mum, my coat.'
'Seriously? It's not cold.'
'I need to check my pockets.'
'Darling, let me do it,' her father offered. 'What
do you need?'
'Don't worry! Just give me the coat!'
Alma squeezed over her
mother's legs, and her father
finally gave her the coat.
She searched the pockets,
the hood and the sleeves.
Nothing. She was getting
desperate. Where could
the baby have gone?
'What have you lost?'
Her father insisted.
Alma was too busy to
answer. She checked her
whole body again.
She took off her shoes
and shook them. Then
she pushed her hands

down her leggings and inside her pants.

She took off her jumper, then her vest.

'Darling, will you tell me what on earth are you doing?' asked her father.

Some nearby passengers were beginning to notice her weird behaviour.

'Alma, cut that out now,' said her father.

He grabbed her vest and tried to pull it back over her head.

'Why are you letting her undress?' her mother asked, getting out of her seat.

'Can't you see I'm trying to dress her? I don't know what's got into her!'

'Oh, you two!' Alma's mother pushed past her father and quickly got her dressed.

Now Alma had looked everywhere.

'Go back to your seat!' her mother said.

But Alma dropped to the floor instead, and started to crawl down the aisle, scanning underneath each seat and between the legs of the passengers. Most of the people found Alma's antics amusing and raised their legs to help her.

'What's she looking for?' one man asked.

'Can I help?' a woman said, a bit annoyed.

It seemed to Alma's mother that half the aeroplane was looking at them.

'It's OK, I'm sure it's nothing important. Please don't mind her,' she answered, embarrassed.

Alma was checking the soles of everyone's shoes, in case the baby had been squashed.

Eventually she stopped and began to cry.

'C'mon, just tell me what you've lost and we'll get you another one,' her mother tried to reassure her, gently leading Alma back to her seat.

Alma curled herself up by the window, sniffling. Slowly, everyone else settled down again.

Quite soon afterwards her mother and father dozed off, resting their heads against each other. But Alma was too upset to sleep. That was when a tiny voice called: 'Ga! Ga!'

Alma immediately turned towards her mother –
and there she was, climbing up her shoulder.
Alma couldn't contain a joyful scream as she
picked up the little girl. Her mother heard it, and
slowly turned her head.
'Darling… you ok…' her mother said – then fell
asleep again.
No one was watching. Alma slowly opened her
hands. The little girl was sitting in her palm.
'Where have you been?' Alma asked her with
relief.
The little girl smiled, wiggled her feet and raised
her arms, as if she wanted to hug Alma.

'Gaaa… Gaaa… Guuu…'

Alma put her finger near her, and the little girl held it affectionately.

Alma raised her to the window and showed her the world outside. There were lots of stars.

'I'm going to take you home with me. We're going to London.'

Chapter 5

Alma's Home

'Time to get up!' Alma heard her mother shout outside her room.

She kicked the duvet off her legs and stretched.

Alma's mother entered her room and pulled opened the curtains.

Alma was still wearing the clothes she had been wearing the day before.

'Here's your breakfast,' her mother said, putting a bowl of cereal on her desk before leaving again.

The dim grey light of a January day lit up her old familiar space. Her table was still covered in pens, books, slime pots and other craft experiments.

Next to her bed was her messy doll's house, her shelves overflowing with books and her old stuffed toys at the very top.

Then, suddenly, she remembered.

'Where's the little girl!?'

Alma jumped off the bed.

'Oh no! I fell asleep. I lost her again!'

She felt her heart pounding.

She searched her bed and pillow, patted her body and her hair.

'Are you eating your breakfast?' her mother called from downstairs.

Alma didn't answer her. Her mind was racing. Then she remembered her coat. Did she put the baby back inside it when she was on the plane? Yes, she did!

The coat was hanging behind her door. She rushed to it, checked her pockets and found the plastic shoe.

She picked it up and looked inside.

And there was the little one, all cuddled up asleep. The sight filled Alma with joy.

'Now… where am I going to put you?'

She had to wear her coat to go to school, so she knew she'd have to leave her in the room somewhere. She looked around.

There was the matryoshka doll… but she could suffocate in there! The pot for her brushes? No, she could climb out of it. Same with her shoes. What about the drawer of her bedside table? That would be perfect.

She cleared some space in the drawer, gingerly placed the shoe inside, and closed it a second before her mother walked in again.

'Haven't you eaten your breakfast yet?' she said.

Alma sat down and quickly emptied the bowl. She had the situation under control.

That morning, she prepared for school in record time. She washed her face, brushed her teeth, combed her hair, checked her school bag, then sat on her bed. She still had five minutes left.

'Why aren't you this quick every day?' her mother asked. Just for once, they wouldn't have a stressful race to school.

Alma was leaning her hand on her bedside cabinet, watching the tiny baby, convinced that she could read her thoughts.

'Don't make any noise today. Just wait here. I'll be back in no time,' she whispered.

When her mother called again, Alma jumped to her feet and rushed to the door, hoping time would go by quickly so that she'd soon return to look after her new friend.

That's right. Her new friend. She still didn't know what to call her, though. She needed a name.

As she walked to school with her mother, Alma didn't say a word.

'You still haven't told me what you lost yesterday on the plane,' her mother asked.

But Alma's mind was busy with more important thoughts.

'I could give her my best friend's name,' she said to herself.

'Mmm. No, that wouldn't be right. And not my name either, that would be too weird! How about a name from one of my Robo-Doll cards? No, this baby needs her own special name. Is she a real girl, anyway? She looks like one, but she's much too small. I found her in an almond, after all… I could call her Almonda. Mmm. It needs to be prettier. Maybe Almondette? Or Almondine? Yes… I like it! That's it. I will call her Almondine.'

And with that thought in mind she skipped and hummed all the way to school.

Chapter 6

Almondine

When Alma came back from school, she rushed to her bedside table and opened the drawer.

'Almondine!?'

Everything inside was in chaos.

Some of Alma's drawings were ripped, her jewellery box had been opened, and beads and rings were scattered everywhere.

'Almondine? What have you done? Come out, where are you?'

The little girl crawled out from under some torn pieces of paper and she was cheerfully holding a scrap in her mouth.

'Pfua!... Ma... Maaaa...' she chuckled, spitting out some of the paper.

'What are you eating?'

'Maaa... Maaa...'

'Mama? Yes, of course. I'm your mama!' Then Alma invited her to repeat 'Maaammmaaa.'

'Maaa... Maaa...mmmma,' Almondine gleefully repeated.

Alma giggled.

'Why were you chewing paper?'

'Mama... ah!' Almondine crawled toward Alma and stretched out her arms.

Alma gently picked her up. Almondine held on to

her finger and then began to suck it.

'So you're hungry! What am I going to give you to eat? Let me think, what do babies eat? Of course, they drink milk! Stay here for one moment. Don't move. And shush!'

Alma gently put Almondine back into the drawer and rushed downstairs.

She came back with a tiny bit of milk in a glass. She poured some of it into one of the vials she used for her slime experiments – after making sure it was a clean one.

She tried to give Almondine some of the milk, but as soon as she tasted it, she started to cry.

'What do you want then? Maybe just water?'

Alma grabbed a teapot from her doll's house, rushed to the bathroom and filled it with water. When she put the spout to Almondine's mouth, the baby stopped crying and drank from it for a surprisingly long time.

'There you go. This is w-a-ter. Hmm… I'll have to teach you how to speak. And… when not to speak!' Almondine carried on drinking and looking

up at Alma with her curious little eyes.

Finally, she took her mouth away from the little teapot and started shaking her limbs with so much energy and enthusiasm that Alma couldn't help laughing out loud.

'You really like water, don't you?' Alma said.

'Ua… a… Ua… a… Ua… a…' the little girl repeated excitedly.

'Bravo. Water, yes. Water. You must be hungry as well… and cold… let me think.'

Then an unexpected voice came from right behind Alma.

'Alma, you are so funny. Talking to your dolls.'

Alma's mother was standing just inside the door of her room.

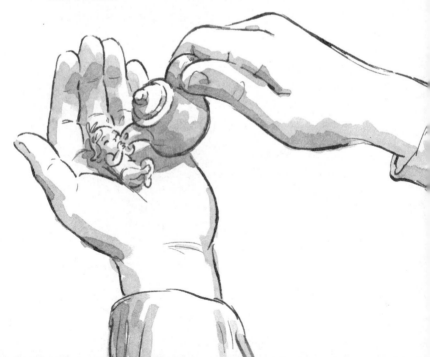

'Mum! Sorry but it's… a private conversation!' Alma said, covering Almondine with her hand.

'I see!' Alma's mother said, smiling. 'All right, I'll leave you to it.' And she walked down the hall.

'Listen – we have to be careful,' Alma told Almondine sternly when her mother had gone. 'No one must see you.'

'Siii… uuuu… Siii… uuuu…'

'That's right. Now, let's find something for you to wear. Tell me, are you cold?'

'Cooold?'

Alma faked a shiver with her shoulders.

'Co…od! Co…od!' Almondine repeated, starting to crawl up Alma's arm.

'Where are you going?'

Alma rolled her back into her hand.

'You don't seem cold... but I need to put something on you. You can't stay naked like this.'
She emptied the pens out of a glass jam jar, then gently set Almondine down on the carpet and put the jar over her.

'Stay there, just for a minute.'

Almondine crawled around inside the jar, trying to find a way out.

Alma shifted her attention to her doll's house and started to sift through all the mess accumulated in weeks of neglect.

At first it seemed that all the dolls' clothes were way too big for Almondine. Then Alma saw a tiny bunny doll wearing a little green dress that might be just perfect for her.

'Almondine, how about this?' Alma said, holding the little dress with two fingers.

But when she turned to show it to Almondine, the baby was staring at a big flowerpot near the doll's house and reaching towards it with one of her tiny hands.

'Why are you looking at that pot?' Alma said.

'Do you want to go there?'

Alma carefully picked her up and put her gently into the flowerpot.

As soon as she touched the soil, Almondine eagerly plunged herself into the damp compost, sinking her mouth into the earth.

'Oh gosh, what are you doing? You can't eat earth! It's not food!'

'Fu... Fu!... Am!... Gnamm...' Almondine replied, her mouth full.

'Whoa... that's gross. Is that what you eat?'

Almondine was gorging on the soil.
'You're so funny! You look like a pig!'
Alma chuckled.
And as she stood enjoying the sight of Almondine happily eating, playing with and rolling in the earth, she forgot what time it was. Then, suddenly her mother called:
'Alma! Have you done your homework?'

Chapter 7

Almondine's Bath

'Alma, remember you only have tomorrow left to do your homework. You didn't touch your exercise book all the time we were away. If you don't, I'll have to tell your father.'

Alma's mother was telling her off while rinsing some dishes in the kitchen sink.

Her father had already left. He was going to be away for three months. Apparently he'd kissed her goodbye in the morning while she was still asleep, but she hadn't noticed.

Now she was humming a tune to herself as she ate her dinner.

She'd put Almondine inside the jam jar and hidden it under the bed, so she had to eat quickly and go back upstairs to make sure the little girl got some fresh air.

Alma checked the clock. Almondine was so dirty from playing in the flowerpot that she should have a good wash, so Alma needed some time before bed to give her a bath.

'Finished!' Leaving her plate half-empty, Alma rushed upstairs.

She closed her bedroom door and reached under the bed for the jam jar. Almondine had curled up inside it, and was sleeping.

'Oh, no. I need to wake you up now. Stay here, we'll be quick.'

Alma delicately placed her filthy Almondine on the table. She wiggled, but kept on sleeping. Alma went to the bathroom to fill the jar with warm water.

She returned to her room and checked the clock. She had about half an hour before her mother would show up again and remind her to get ready for bed.

'Wakey, wakey…' Alma tickled Almondine with her finger. Almondine giggled happily and opened her eyes.
'Mama,' she called with her tiny voice.
'Are you ready for a bath, sweetie?'
Ignoring Alma's question, Almondine started to crawl around the table.
Alma picked her up with two fingers and delicately dropped her in the water.
Almondine swiftly swam under the water and didn't seem to be willing to come back up.
'Oh no, you are going to drown like that!'
Alma grabbed the jar and poured some water back into the flowerpot. Almondine slipped out and

fell into a muddy puddle.

'Oops! Sorry.' Alma tried to pick her up again but Almondine got to her feet and stomped happily about in the mud.

'Look at you – you can stand now!'

But just as Alma said that, Almondine fell flat on her face.

'Oh dear, that's enough. Come here – it's time to finish your bath now.'

Alma picked up Almondine and put her inside the near-empty jar of water.

She placed it on the desk and watched, amused, as the baby splashed and rolled inside the jar, getting clean at the same time. Alma's lamp was the only light in the room, shining like a spotlight on Almondine.

Time flew in the darkness.

'Are you ready for bed?' Alma's mother called from downstairs.

'Oh no! Come here, Almondine.'
Alma squeezed her hand inside the jar, picked
Almondine up with two fingers and put her on a
paper tissue to dry. Then she took a grey woolly
hat from one of her big dolls and tucked
Almondine inside it.
'Now you have to stay here – and shush, OK?'
'Shhhhhh!'
'That's right. Shush.'
Her mother suddenly opened the door.
'You haven't got your pyjamas on!'
Alma had just closed the drawer of the bedside
table in time.
'What's this dirty water doing on your table? You
know I don't like you playing with water in your

room. That's what the garden's for. Off you go. Get ready for bed.'

Her mother took the jar away and went to the bathroom to empty it.

From inside the bedside table, Alma heard her faint voice:

'Shhhhh... Shhhhhhhh...'

She quickly opened the drawer.

'Shut up! Can't you be quiet?'

'Clo... yoo... mau!... shhhhh...'

'Stop that, you have to go to sleep now.'

'Alma? Who are you talking to now?' her mother asked as she put the clean jar back on the table. 'You're getting a bit too old for this nonsense. Go and brush your teeth, now.'

Alma made sure her mother left the room with her as she headed for the bathroom.
When she'd finished her teeth, hands and face, she walked back to her room.

Her mother was looking in her drawer.

Chapter 8

Alma's Homework

'Mum! You're not allowed! These are my things,' Alma shouted, running to stand between her mother and the bedside table.

'When are you going to tidy up this mess?'

'I will.'

'Look at the time!'

Luckily, it seemed she hadn't found Almondine. Alma quickly put on her pyjamas and went to bed. 'Would you like me to read you a quick story before we switch off the light?' asked her mum. Alma would have loved that, but she wanted to make sure that Almondine remained safe.

'Not tonight, Mum, thanks; I'm sleepy.'

Alma switched off her night-light.

'You are becoming a big girl,' her mother said as she kissed her goodnight. Alma didn't kiss her back as usual.

'Night,' she replied simply.

Her mother left the room and closed the door behind her.

Alma waited a few minutes, then reached for the little rocket torch on her bedside table which she sometimes used to find the toilet at night. She shone the light on to the ceiling, then gently opened the drawer. She could see Almondine

61

sleeping cosily, huddled up in the woolly hat at the end of the drawer.

'Good night, Almondine,' she said softly.

She carefully closed the drawer, switched off the light and went to sleep.

The next day, Alma skipped and hopped her way back from school.

'You remember what you have to do this afternoon, don't you?' asked her mother, hurrying behind her.

Alma knew her homework was due the next day.

They were studying the Greek gods, and she had to draw one of the twelve Olympians and describe their life.

As soon as she got home, she sat down at her desk, cleared some space and took a big notebook out of her bag. Then she wrote 'ATHENA' in big letters at the top of a blank page.

She sucked the end of the pencil and turned to look at the drawer. Was Almondine still there? She must be. And she was quiet – probably asleep. If she were to wake her up now, it would be difficult to finish her homework. Thinking back to the lesson, she began

to write about how brave and wise and strong Athena was.

She remembered the story of how Athena was born, by jumping out of Zeus's cracked head. Alma thought that was funny. She decided to draw this moment: an old, bearded man with his head split in half and Athena gloriously bursting out of it.

She took her box of watercolours and brush, and unzipped her pencil case. She was now ready to sketch the picture. But just when she was about to start, she heard a noise from the drawer.

'Are you awake?!' Alma jumped off her chair and opened the drawer.

'Mama…'

Almondine had got out of the woolly hat, and when Alma pulled the drawer open she fell back on her behind.

'Oops! Sorry,' said Alma.

Almondine stood up; she was still naked.

Alma remembered the cute little dress she'd found the day before, and how Almondine had not even worn it yet.

'Here, put this on.'

She gently helped her into it.

Almondine loved herself decorated in this pretty piece of green fabric. Then she pointed to her mouth and said: 'Foo… gnam… gnam.' 'Oh my baby, of course you're hungry again! But you mustn't get messy now.' Alma picked up a little plastic spoon and gave the girl a morsel of the soil from the pot.

Almondine seemed to
like it very much.
Then she gave her
some water from
the small toy
teapot until she
seemed perfectly
content and satisfied.
'Now, come here. Look
at what I'm doing.'

Alma picked her up and put her on her table next
to the notebook.

'Stay there and watch. I'm going to draw Athena.'

Almondine's first reaction was to try to tear off the
corner of the page.

Alma told her off, and Almondine sat down, a
little confused.

Alma started to draw passionately, explaining the
meaning of every stroke to Almondine.

At first she stood still and watched the marks
appearing on the page, as if by magic.

Then she got up and walked around the
notebook, exploring what Alma was drawing.

Recognising a pretty girl with a dress similar to her
own, she walked over to her and started to jump
and babble excitedly.

'Almondine, stay here.' Alma gently nudged her to one side. 'Yes, she does look like you.' Alma playfully touched Almondine's chest with a finger.

'Eeuuu!' Almondine copied, pointing at Alma.

'No, you… You.' Alma pointed at Almondine.

'Eeuuu!' Almondine pointed at herself.

'No, you have to say ME.' Alma tapped her own chest.

'Meee!' Almondine shouted happily, pointing at Alma now.

'No, I'm ME, you is for YOU.' Alma pointed back at Almondine.

Almondine was puzzled. Was it a game? She swayed and giggled merrily.

'OK. I'm Alma. I am YOU. For you.' Alma pointed to Almondine 'Me, Almondine.'

'Meee. Ammodeee!'

'Yes! You are Almondine!' Alma clapped.

'I'm Alma.'

'Mamma…'

'Well... yes. I'm that as well.' Alma was overjoyed. Almondine was picking up a few words!

'Now, I need to finish my picture by painting in some colours.'

She dipped her brush in the water and wet the ten watercolours in their tray which had been left so dirty, they all looked the same dark brown. Soon, as each wet stroke cleaned the surface, vivid colours started to emerge. All this delighted Almondine, as if it was a magic trick.

'Alma! Your father wants to say hi,' her mother called from outside the room. 'Come quickly!'

'Not now,' Alma complained to herself.

She picked up a book, half opened it and put it against the wall. Then she put Almondine behind it, to stop her from leaving.

'Stay here; I'll be quick.'

Alma rushed out of the room. She wanted it to be a quick hello and goodbye, but her mother held her arm, insisting that she kept talking to her father. As much as Alma loved spending time with her father, talking long-distance wasn't that much fun, but most of all, she had more important things to do.

Finally, her mother let her go, and she ran back to her room.

She must have been away longer than she thought. Almondine was crawling over the picture, completely covered in watercolour paint.

'Oh, no! What have you done?'

There were smudges and smears, hand and footprints in every colour, all over the page.

As soon as Almondine saw Alma, she got on to her feet and started to jump up and down.

'Amondee! Amondee!'

'Stop that!'

Alma picked her up, washed her in the water bowl, pulled a paper tissue from the box and put her inside it.

'Naughty Almondine. You were supposed to wait
for me. Naughty!'
'Nodeee! Nodeee!' Almondine replied, all excited.
'I'll need to find another dress for you.'

Then she looked at the picture. It was a dreadful
sight. How was she going to present this mess at
school for 'Show and Tell'?

Chapter 9

Almondine's Drawings

When Alma presented her picture to the class, everyone sniggered. She'd tried to rescue the drawing by repainting some parts and tracing over some of the writing, but it hadn't worked.

'Interesting rendition. Thank you, Alma,' said Miss Maynard, her teacher, obviously unimpressed. 'But please try to be more precise next time. You shouldn't be playing while doing your homework.'

When Alma dejectedly returned to her desk, her best friend Leonor told her she loved it.

'It's so cool – it looks like a volcanic explosion.

What did you use to make these cute little hand and footprints?'

'Do you like them? I used some… Well, I didn't use anything, I… Actually, it's a secret.'

'A secret?'

'One day I'll tell you, but you'll have to promise me not to tell anyone, OK?'

After school, Alma went to her room.

Opening the door, she heard a feeble sob coming from the drawer.

Alma stood Almondine on her hand. She was still wearing her flowery dress from the bunny toy. She had been chewing on its skirt and looked upset.

'Mama… foo…
foo… foo…'
'Of course, I'm
so sorry, sweetie.'
Alma gave
Almondine her usual meal
of earth and a teapot of water,
but it didn't cheer her up much.
'Why are you so sad? Come on – let's play a bit.'
Alma put her in the doll's house. It was too big for
Almondine. Most of Alma's dolls looked gigantic
next to her, except for a couple of smaller ones and
some little bunnies.
Alma took one of the bunnies and play-acted a
little scene, holding it with two fingers.
She put on a high-pitched voice and
tried to encourage Almondine to
play along.
But Almondine didn't find it fun.
She frowned at the bunny.
When Alma insisted, poking her
gently with the bunny's paws,
Almondine turned away and
tried to find a hiding-place in the
living room of the doll's house.
'Come on, Almondine, let's play.'

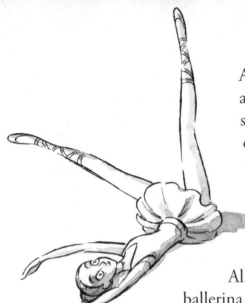

Almondine backed away as Alma moved a small plastic princess close to her, then gave the doll a slap. Alma offered her a little ballerina with one leg raised. That was even worse. Almondine grabbed the ballerina with both hands and threw her down the doll's house stairs.

Almondine ran to the other side of the doll's house, where small clothes were messily scattered on top of each other.

She threw herself on top of them.

'Nodee… Nodee… Amondin nodee…'

'No, you are not naughty. Just tell me what you want to play with. Let's do something together.'

'Nodeee,' Almondine insisted, pointing at her desk.

Alma's colouring set was still there from her homework the day before.

Alma took a small piece of white paper and some pencil-stumps and placed them on the floor of the doll's house.

Almondine's face brightened. She grabbed
one of the pencils, and, hugging it like a
huge log, tried to scribble some lines. It
was too big for her.

'Nodeee… Nodeee…' Almondine
stopped and pointed back at the
table again.

'Do you want the
watercolours?'

'Uadecolo… Uadecolo…'
Alma wetted all the
watercolours and put
the box in the doll's house.
Almondine became very
excited. She rolled in the
colours, then hopped around
the page. She began to clap her hands and stamp
her feet. She wriggled her body and made clumsy
roly-polies, leaving weird, abstract pictures on the
page. Alma liked these creations, and swapped the
sheet for a clean one every now and then.

Alma looked at the doll's house, trying to figure
out how she could make it into a proper home for
Almondine. It needed to be safe, and to have a
good place to hide if Alma's mum came in.

How could she make sure she kept her little friend

secret? Almondine was very energetic, and over the last few days she'd shown that she could get almost anywhere she wanted to.

Alma decided the drawer was still the safest place to hide her.

But would Almondine be too restless to stay there when Alma wasn't home?

Chapter 10

Bedtime Stories

Alma wanted Almondine to have a home, but the wilful little girl didn't seem very interested.

Nevertheless, Alma cut out some white cotton sheets and made five curtains, one for each room of the doll's house. For the living room she even cut out a tiny window. Then she stitched some blue ribbons next to the curtains so they could stay parted when she was playing with Almondine, but could also be drawn quickly if she needed to hide her from view. She added some pegs to keep the sheets taut and secure.

It was a fine job, which took her several days to

prepare. And even her mother was impressed with the result.

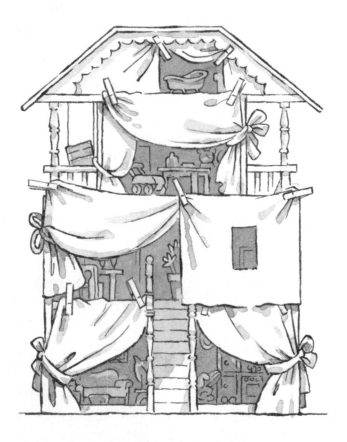

Almondine seemed to like what Alma had done, but she was still more relaxed in the flowerpot. Soon, though, even that began to bore her. She wanted to explore, rather than spending time

playing in one place. Almondine was growing fast, and becoming more and more restless and inquisitive. She was also learning more words, but she often misunderstood their meanings. Alma found her irresistible, even when she was a bit naughty. The evenings were always tricky, because it was then that Alma's mother invaded her room, and Alma had to make sure Almondine stayed hidden.

One night, Alma's mother insisted that she should read her a story. She was worried that her daughter had become so evasive lately, and she wanted to spend more time with Alma and find out what she was thinking about.

Alma gave Almondine a pep-talk at her bedside table.

'Stay here, and remember, not a word… shush…'

'Shush… shush…' Almondine repeated, looking a little miserable.

'You can listen, too. Just be good in there.'

Alma pushed the drawer, leaving it slightly ajar.

Alma's mother came in, sat on her bed, opened a Peter Rabbit book and started to read The Tale of Mr Tod. Her mother probably liked Peter Rabbit more than Alma did, and this particular story was a bit scary.

Almondine was also listening to Alma's mother's reading. It sounded interesting, so she peeked her little head out of the drawer.

The light was dim. Alma and her mother were leaning against a pillow at the end of the bed. Whatever they were looking at, Almondine thought it must be fascinating.

She squeezed out of the drawer and began to make her way across the duvet towards them.

The story was nearly finished when Alma felt a little tickle creeping up her shoulder. She was about to scream but clenched her teeth when she turned and saw Almondine leaning over, staring at the open page. She could only hope the little girl would keep quiet and so she waited until her mother turned the last page of the story.

'Now, little rabbit, time for you to sleep,' her mother said.

Alma quickly grabbed her pillow and turned away to get under the duvet and hide Almondine but

when she checked her shoulder again she was no
longer there.

'What are you looking for?' asked her mother after
getting up.

'Nothing, good night,' she said, tucking herself
under and turning to face the wall.

'Good night, sleepy head,' said her mother giving
her a kiss.

Alma closed her eyes and just waited for her to
leave the room and turn off the light.

Finally her mum left and closed the door.

Alma counted up to five, then turned on her torch.
'Almondine, where are you? Did I squish you?'
She lifted the duvet and the pillow. Then she got
off the mattress and squeezed under the bed,
shining her torch around.
There were lots of long-lost treasures down there.
Alma pushed a big box aside and squeezed
through a little further.
'There you are!'
Almondine was near the skirting board, cowering
away from an old rubber Tyrannosaurus rex.
'Come here.' Alma reached out for her hand.
The door opened, and light from the corridor
shone in the room.

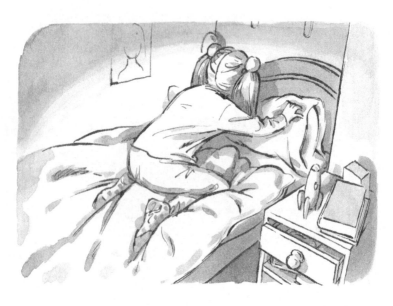

'Did you pee before going to bed?'
Alma banged her head against the bed frame.
'Alma! What are you doing under the bed!?'
'Just stay there,' Alma whispered to Almondine.
Alma switched off the torch and came out.
'What are you looking for? I've never heard of a
girl crawling under the bed at night!'
Alma rushed to the toilet, faked having a pee and
rushed back.
'Goodnight, Mum, you can go now.'
Her mother stroked her head.
'Try to sleep now.'
Her mother left and closed the door. Alma

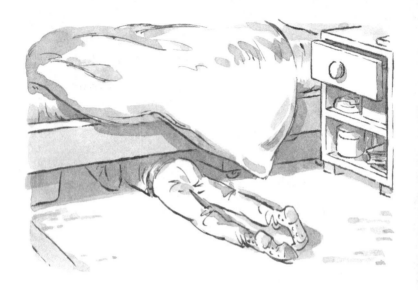

counted again until five. Then:

'Almondine? Are you still there?'

Alma squeezed her arm between the bed and the wall and reached down, until she felt tiny hands gripping one of her fingers.

When she pulled Almondine up and turned on the torch, she was covered with dust. Alma blew on her, which Almondine found funny and immediately blew back at her.

'You should have waited in here; wasn't that what I told you?'

Alma said as she put her back in the drawer. Almondine kept blowing at her, wanting to play.

'Now, you go to sleep, too.' Alma got back to bed, turned over and tried to sleep, but she could hear Almondine repeating words from the story and noisily rummaging about inside the bedside table.

Chapter 11

Fun at Night

It was the beginning of a new routine.

Now Almondine wanted a bedtime story every night, and Alma decided to read it to her herself instead of letting her mother do it. Having her in the room was too risky.

This was how Almondine learned to talk, and discovered more about the outside world.

Alma would open the book on her lap, and Almondine would stand on top of the pages, often interrupting Alma to ask questions about the story or the illustrations.

They both enjoyed playing games with colours,

spending hours scribbling and painting. Sometimes, Alma traced the outline of Almondine's body, and they both drew and coloured different dresses on to it. Or Alma would make a thumbprint on the paper with paint for Almondine to draw a face inside.

Sometimes Alma would put Almondine into the pencil sharpener tray. Almondine loved being in there, with all the colourful shavings. She reminded Alma of her best friend's hamster. But Almondine was a lot cleverer, and didn't need a cage. Or did she? Alma wondered sometimes.

All this fun was beginning to have consequences for Alma.

Almondine was a force of nature, and she didn't seem to get tired, especially as time went on.

In the evenings she was becoming more and more stubborn when it was time for bed.

One night, Almondine didn't want to sleep at all and, despite countless lullabies, she kept moaning in her drawer.

'Gosh, it's so hard to have a baby!' Alma complained. Her eyes felt heavy.

Alma turned on her torch, picked Almondine up and put her on the bed.

'What's wrong with you tonight? You are being simply unbearable.'

'Anada storee.'

'Almondine, it's late. I'm sleepy.'

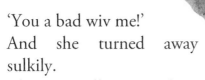

'You a bad wiv me!'
And she turned away
sulkily.
Alma was still pointing her torch
towards her, casting a shadow on the
wall. Almondine looked at it. She moved –
and the shadow moved. She turned to Alma
and pointed at it.
'Wad is da?'
'It's your shadow.' She couldn't have ever noticed
it before. 'OK, look.'
Alma put the torch down on the duvet and used
her hands to cast the shadow of a duck's head on
the wall.

'You see, I can do that, or this,'
she said adjusting her fingers to
form a dog's profile. 'Woof!'
It was so big that Almondine
was a bit scared at first, but then
she loved it. She stepped into

the circle of torchlight and pretended to play with the dog. Alma found it funny, and forgot to sleep for a long while.

After that, Alma had to make up endless new games every night so that Almondine would get tired and fall asleep, which happened later and later every time.

Until one night they fell asleep together on the bed, with the torch still on.

Chapter 12

Too Much for Alma

'Alma! Time to wake up!'
Alma managed to hide Almondine in her fist just before her mother arrived at her bedside to give her a morning kiss.
That was close, she thought.
She got up and walked to the bathroom.
Closing the door, she opened her fist and placed Almondine on the side of the sink.
'Almondine, we have to be more careful,' said Alma while sitting on the loo.
Her heavy eyelids closed for one last brief moment of sleep.

Meanwhile, Almondine slid her hands over the slippery soap. She didn't like the smell, or the feeling of it on her fingers. She climbed over the spout and tried to wash it off her hands from the dripping tap. Then she noticed some curious brushes and a big tube of paint.

A loud SMASH finally woke Alma up.

Almondine had fallen into the sink with the toothbrushes and toothpaste, shattering the pretty pot holding them.

'Almondine!! Be careful. Why don't you ever stop?' Alma cried.

She rushed to the sink and saved the little girl from slipping down the drain.

'Are you OK, darling?' Alma's mother called, hearing the noise. 'Open the door! You know I don't like you locking yourself in. What have you broken in there?'

'I'm coming!' Alma answered, after putting Almondine next to the soap tray.

She tried to tidy up the mess but it was useless, so she left it all on the side of the sink.

'Alma? Open the door.'

Alma picked Almondine up and put her on her shoulder, under her pyjamas.

'Don't move, or you'll tickle me!'

Alma opened the bathroom door.

'I'm sorry, Mum, it was my fault. It was an accident.'

'Listen to me, young lady. You have to tell me what's going on with you. You don't sleep at night, you don't do your homework, you're always talking to yourself...' As her mother reproached her, Alma could feel Almondine climbing down her leg.

'You don't talk to me any more. You stay in your room all the time... I'm worried about you,' her mum insisted.

Almondine jumped down from Alma's foot and

dashed out of the bathroom, excitedly darting across the landing and running towards Alma's mother's bedroom.

'Sorry, Mum!'

Alma dashed off too.

'Alma, come here! Talk to me!'

Alma ran to her mother's bedroom and saw Almondine disappearing among her shoes.

She kneeled down and started to check each one.

'Almondine! Where are you? This isn't funny.'

'What are you up to now, Alma? Why are you looking at my shoes? Why are you so weird?!'

Alma saw Almondine hopping about inside the small wicker bin next to the shoes.

She picked up the bin and left the bedroom.

'Where are you going with that now? Leave it.'

Alma went to her room with the bin, closed the door and quickly searched through crumpled paper and scraps until she found Almondine cheerfully looking up at her. Alma

grabbed her and put her in the drawer just as her mum reopened the door.

'What are you doing with my bin in your room? Listen, I don't want you to close this door any more if you carry on like this! I wish your dad was here to see how you're behaving…'

Alma sat on her bed and listened to her mother on full blast. But at least Almondine was safe.

This was just one day in Alma's life. She was always covering up Almondine's mischief.

She couldn't focus on much else, so she wasn't doing very well at school. It got worse every day. Miss Maynard couldn't help noticing the change in Alma, and how she often seemed tired.

One afternoon after school, her mother sat her down in the dining room.

'I've had a talk with your teacher, Alma. She says you're not following the lessons properly, and she's seen you falling asleep in class twice. Tell me what's wrong.'

Her voice was quiet, but very serious.

'Nothing.' Alma tried to brush her off.

'Tell me the truth, Alma. Do you think I haven't noticed it, too?'

Alma stared at her mother.

'Alma, is there anything you want to tell me?'

'What do you mean?'

'You've got something secret in your room, haven't you?'

'No, I haven't!'

'I know there's something going on in there. You're always talking to someone,' her mother said with a slight smile. 'I need you to tell me if it's troubling you.'

Oh no… she's found out! Alma thought, *She must know about Almondine, and now she wants me to admit it and tell her. Has she really found her?*

Chapter 13

The Socket

'Almondine, has Mum seen you?' Alma whispered to Almondine, as she lifted her out of the drawer.

She'd tried to sidestep her mother's questions, but she needed to find out just what had happened. She'd shut herself in her room again, but she knew her mother wasn't going to tolerate that for long.

'Maee mum! I love you...' the little girl replied with a big smile.

'Yes, me too. But my mum, MY mum, did she see you when I wasn't here, when I was at school?'

'Big mummee? I don like her. She shout.'

'I know. But I need to find out if she's seen you, do you understand? Did she open this drawer?'

'Yes. She open. Saw her big eyes. Anghee eyes.'

'Oh no! She's seen you, then! Has she? Tell me, did she really see you?'

'Don know,' Almondine shrugged. 'Let's play!'

Almondine jumped off her hand, landed on the carpet with a tumble and ran off.

'Stay here! Did she talk to you? Did she pick you up? What happened?'

Almondine scurried towards the corner where Alma kept her shoes.

'Almondine, it's important. Answer me!'

Almondine grabbed Alma's toy fire engine and pushed it under the wardrobe.

That's it, Alma thought to herself. *She must have seen you. Maybe I should talk to her now.*

Almondine emerged from the other end of the wardrobe with a crochet needle.

She'll just freak out. Or maybe not. Maybe I can convince her to help me keep you here... in my room... and keep you safe.

Almondine was making her way towards the wall with the big needle.

'Let's draw!'

'That's not for drawing.'

Alma wondered how many other things had accumulated under the wardrobe. Now Almondine was near an electric socket. She seemed to notice it for the first time.

'What is dat?'

She banged the needle on the plastic cover, then tried to squeeze it into one of the holes.

'Stop!! Are you mad?!' Alma threw herself at Almondine and snatched the needle from her just in time.

'Don't do that! Ever! Do you undersand? It's very, very dangerous!' Alma shouted. 'Do you get it?'

Almondine watched her reaction with a mixture of shock and amusement.

'I must hide this needle.' As she looked around for a good place, Almondine observed the electric sockets's holes, intrigued.

'Almondine, I'm serious!' Almondine turned, put her hands behind her and smiled.

'It's dangerous. Wait there.' Alma climbed on her

chair, searching for her knitting box.

'There's electricity in it. Let me explain what would happen if…'

Almondine had disappeared.

'Where are you now? Huff…'

Alma left the crochet needle up on a shelf.

When she jumped down from the chair, Almondine had already pulled the fire engine near the sockets and was climbing on its ladder towards the holes. 'Stop!' Alma gasped, lunging for Almondine. The little girl simply laughed.

She was teasing Alma; it was all just a game for her. Alma immediately picked up the fire engine and

put it back on her desk. 'You're not going to use this ladder, either.' Her mother's voice came from behind the door.

'Alma? Who are you talking to, again?' Alma gestured to Almondine to hide under the wardrobe.

'Nobody! Just playing, Mum,' Alma said.

She sat on the floor, legs crossed, trying to look innocent. Her mother opened the door.

'What sort of playing? I heard you shouting that something was dangerous.'

'Mum,' Alma pouted, 'are you spying on me?'

'No, I'm not. But you need to keep this door open. Anyway, come with me and help fold the clothes.'

'I can't, Mum. Why can't you do it yourself?'
Alma grumbled.

'Why can't you? You're just sitting there, doing
nothing. Come on, out of this room.'

'The clothes are on my bed,' her mother said,
heading out.

Alma followed her, but before leaving her room
she looked back and saw Almondine peeping out
from under the wardrobe.

Alma placed her index finger to her lips.

'Be good,' she whispered, and closed the door.

Almondine looked around the room. She was
alone and free. She could barely hear Alma's

103

mother behind the wall.

She looked at the socket again. What was so special about those holes?

She placed a slipper against the wall and climbed up. She stared inside the holes again.

Then she decided it was a good idea to reach inside one of the holes and catch a piece of electricity.

Chapter 14

Almondine is Dead

Alma had just finished helping her mother fold up the sheets when the lights went off.

Alma immediately guessed what had happened. She found her way back to her room in the dark, while her mother went down to the fuse-box near the front door.

Alma tiptoed to her bedside table, trying not to step on anything.

She turned on her torch and shone it straight at the socket. Almondine was lying next to Alma's flip flops. She wasn't moving, and there was a wisp of

smoke in the air.
Alma picked
her up,
begging her
to wake up.
Almondine
was as stiff as a
porcelain statuette.
Her left arm was still held
up high, her fingers splayed.
The lights came back on.
'It was from the upstairs sockets,'
mother said as she walked back up. 'I'm
quite sure I didn't leave the iron on.'
'Alma, did you plug anything in?' her mum
asked as she entered her room. 'Were you using
those 3D pens, or…' she stopped when she saw
Alma kneeling on the carpet next to the socket and
holding what looked like a model of a little girl.
'Alma, was that you, then? Did you put something
in that socket?'
She checked the socket, not really looking at what
Alma was holding in her hand, and turned off the
little red switch.
'See this switch? It needs to be off. The red sticker
should be hidden, like this.' She switched it off.

'All the time. Do you understand?'

Alma was sobbing, standing with her hands clasped.

'Darling, it's OK. Nothing's happened.' Alma's mother hugged her. 'Were you scared?'

Alma felt her mother's hand gently stroking her head and shoulder.

'What have you got there?' her mother asked.

Alma was still holding Almondine.

'She's dead,' Alma cried.

'Who's dead? This little doll?' her mother sighed, 'Come downstairs, now. It's time for dinner.'

Mum took Almondine from her as if she were any other toy and put her in the doll's house bed.

Then, she took Alma by the hand and they both left the room.

That evening Alma tried to bring Almondine back to life. She moistened her, warmed her in a blanket, stroked her, kissed her and hugged her but nothing seemed to work. It looked like her special friend was dead and gone.

She felt guilty that she had left her alone, that she had been unable to keep her safe.

She went to bed with Almondine lying on her pillow, and sobbed herself to sleep.

Chapter 15

Outside

When Alma woke up the next morning, Almondine wasn't on the pillow any more.

Alma searched her bed, and when she still couldn't find her, she looked around the room. There she was! In the flowerpot, eating soil.

'You're alive! You're alive!'

'Who's alive, darling?' her mother asked from outside the room.

'Almondine, how are you feeling?' Alma whispered, kneeling next to the pot.

'Head… hurt…' Almondine replied with her mouth full, still chewing.

'Come here.'
Alma picked her up
and examined her.
Almondine sat down in
her hand. She wasn't
looking too well, but
at least she was alive
– that was all that
really mattered.
'I'll look after you,
don't worry.'

That day at school, Alma was so happy that she wanted to tell the whole world about Almondine, especially her best friend Leonor. She'd already told her that she had a secret. She could invite her over, but that would take time to organise.
She decided to bring Almondine to school, but the next day she still wasn't feeling well; she needed more time to recover before she could leave the house safely.

Alma thought it was good for Almondine to get some sunlight, so she'd often put her by the window. That was how Almondine started to become interested in the outside world, especially their back garden.

'Would you like me to take you outside into the garden, Almondine?'

'Yes! We go outside.'

'OK. But don't run away. Promise you won't.'

'Promise.'

Almondine seemed to have calmed down a bit since the shock. Alma thought this might be because she was still recovering. But Almondine was growing. She didn't look like a toddler any more. In fact she looked about the same age as Alma, but very much smaller!

With Almondine on her shoulder, Alma opened the back door and walked into the garden.

'Here we are.'

Daffodils were growing beside the lawn, and the

stems of the first bluebells were appearing; the mimosa tree was still laden with fluffy yellow flowers, and there were long pink buds on the magnolia. Early bumblebees were buzzing from one flower to another and Spritz, the neighbour's cat, was enjoying the sun on one of their garden chairs. It was springtime.

Almondine found all these sights so amazing that she was speechless.

A couple of years back, Alma's father had built her a little playhouse. She'd only really used it for making slime, and other messy experiments. But now it could become their special hiding place in the garden.

'When it's warmer we can play here,' Alma said, opening the door.

There was a long shelf with lots of pots standing on it. Underneath it, two snails were firmly stuck to a small green chair. And there was her old pink bicycle, a pump, a deflated ball, some buckets and other forgotten objects. As Alma ventured in, cobwebs brushed her face.

'Yaaak!'

Alma hated spiders, so she shook her head and slapped her hair.

'We can't play here yet, Almondine. We need to clean this place first.' Alma said, stroking her face. She felt the cat rubbing the back of her leg.

'Hey, Spritz,' Alma said as she squatted. 'Would you like to meet my friend, Almondine?'

Almondine was unsure about the strange new creature, and had climbed up Alma's shoulder.

The cat didn't care, and kept butting Alma's leg with his head.

'He's cute, isn't he? He's a Persian, that's why he's so fluffy.' Alma patted his head and scratched under his chin.

Then the cat looked up at Alma, and saw

Almondine. He widened his lazy blue eyes, gave a meow and bent his ears back.

'Let's go back inside. Tomorrow you'll have another new experience. I'm taking you to school with me!'

Chapter 16

Almondine at School

Alma walked to school with her right hand firmly inside her pocket, holding the grey woolly hat with Almondine inside. It was a cool spring day and she wanted to make sure Almondine was warm, safe and cosy.

In class she hung up her coat and secretly placed the woolly bundle, with Almondine inside, in the big front pocket of her dress.

Recently, she'd been made to sit next to Tom. He definitely wasn't going to see Almondine. Her best friend, Leonor, was sitting across the room. She waved at her and, pointing to her pocket,

indicated that she'd show her something later.
Leonor did the same; she had something to show Alma, too.

The class passed slowly.

Every now and then Alma checked on Almondine, who was peeping out of the pocket and looking around.

'Look, but don't move. I'll take you out when it's break time,' she whispered.

'Alma! Are you listening?'

'Yes, Miss Maynard. Sorry.'

'Pay attention to what I'm saying, Alma, because I'm going to ask you to repeat it later.'

The bell rang for break. Alma got up and went over to Leonor.

'I need to show you something.'

'Me too!' Leonor said, excitedly. 'Look.' She pulled out a plastic ball and popped it open.

Inside there was a cool Robo-Doll: the one Leonor needed to complete her collection. Alma loved them as well but they were quite expensive and she only had two. Now, not even her card collection could compare with what she had discovered.

'Come on, let's play!' Leonor called another couple of friends over, and ran into the hallway. Alma needed a quiet moment to show Almondine

to Leonor. There were too many girls around
them, all eager to play with the Robo-Doll.

The bell rang again and the rest of the kids raced
back to the classroom.

'Leonor…' Alma grabbed her hand. 'I wanted to
show you something too.'

'What is it?'

'It's in my pocket, come closer. Look.'

'Alma, Leonor,' Miss Maynard said while
standing at the door, 'time to get back in. Class
starts now.'

'Show me at lunch, OK?' Leonor said.

Inside the classroom, the boys were chasing each

other around the tables. Just as Alma was approaching her seat, Tom bashed into her from behind.

To stop herself from falling, Alma pulled her hands out of her pocket and grabbed on to the table. The woolly hat fell to the floor with Almondine inside it and started to scurry through tables and chairs, and between the legs of the kids.

'A mouse!' one boy shouted.

'I saw it! Over there!' screamed another.

'Ahh!' shrieked another girl.

'Help!' another one jumped on her chair.

Suddenly the whole class was in a state of panic. Almondine zigzagged under a chest of drawers. Alma immediately kneeled down and tried to look under it. Other kids joined her.

'Can you see it?' one of them enquired.

'Go away!' Alma replied and stretched her arm under it whispering: 'Come back here, it's me.'

'Let's get a stick and whack it!' shouted Tom.

'Here, use this ruler!'

'Are you all mad!' Alma cried.

Miss Maynard came to bring order to the commotion, but she was a little uneasy herself.

'Calm down, everyone,' she said out loud. 'A mouse won't hurt anybody. It's more scared than

you. Sit down and let's carry on with the class. We'll sort this out later.'

Alma felt a bit guilty to have accidentally caused this situation, and most of all she was terribly worried about Almondine.

Finally the kids settled down and the lesson carried on, but Alma could not take her eyes off the little gap under the drawers.

It seemed as if lunchtime would never arrive.

Chapter 17

The Mouse

When the bell rang for lunchtime most of the kids rushed out of the door, but some of the boys stayed inside to check under the gap again.

'Come on. Everyone out!' Miss Maynard said. 'You too, Alma.'

In the dining hall, Alma sat alone, struggling to eat anything. Leonor sat next to her.

'What did you want to show me? Don't tell me you have a Robo-Doll as well!'

'No.'

'You look upset.'

Alma didn't know how to explain what had

happened. It would sound as if she'd made it up. All she cared about was getting Almondine back. She wished she'd left her at home but now it was too late. She could not wait around any longer. 'See you in a bit, Leonor,' she said, and left the hall.

Back in the classroom, she found Mr Hale, the caretaker, pulling the chest of drawers away from the wall. Miss Maynard was standing next to him with a broom. 'No!' Alma shouted. 'Don't hurt her!' 'Alma, what are you doing here? Why aren't you in the hall with the others, eating your lunch?'

'Did you see anything behind there?' Mr Hale asked Miss Maynard.

'No,' she replied, looking at the gap again.

The caretaker knelt down and reached behind the chest of drawers. When he pulled his arm out, he was holding a couple of pencils and the woolly hat.

'That's mine!' Alma rushed to say.

She picked up the hat, brushed some dust off it and put it in her pocket. Then she walked around the room, looking at the floor and whispering: 'Almondine? Where are you?'

'We'll put out some poison later,' Mr Hale said, 'but we'll need to find out how it got in.'

The bell rang again, and the kids started to take their seats.

Everyone seemed to have forgotten about the incident.

But Alma kept on desperately scanning the place for any sign of Almondine.

Then, by chance, she spotted her in an unexpected place: on the highest shelf in the room, and exploring some cardboard Trojan horses that the children

had made a few weeks earlier. Miss Maynard had put them out of reach to keep them safe.

Alma tried to hide her relief. She hoped that nobody else had spotted Almondine, or it could be the end of her tiny friend.

Almondine waved to her and Alma opened her eyes wide, secretly signalling her to keep quiet and wait for her.

When class ended, everybody rushed out to meet their parents. Alma stayed behind, and when she checked the Trojan horses, she couldn't see

Almondine any more. How was she going to find her without anybody noticing?

Then she heard Miss Maynard's voice saying something surprising.

'Your dad's here for you, Alma.'

Chapter 18

The Bicycle

'Dad?'

It was true. There was her father standing outside the classroom. He had already started to talk to Miss Maynard. There was no time to waste, Alma needed to find Almondine right away.

'Come out, quickly! Where are you?'

'Here, Mummy!' Almondine peeked from behind the box for the water bottles.

'There you are! How did you get there?' Alma swiftly picked her up and hid her in a pocket.

Relieved, Alma walked out of the classroom and gave her father a big hug.

On the way home, he asked a lot of questions, but seemed particularly interested in why her mother was so worried about her. Alma didn't say much; she just wanted to get home and put Almondine back in her drawer.

The little girl was a bit sad to be hidden away, but Alma insisted.

'Stay there. Don't make a noise, and don't say a thing. Dad's here. I'll come back later.'

Before closing the drawer, Alma called her once more.

'Almondine…'

The little girl turned.

'I love you very much,' Alma told her with a smile. Almondine smiled, and Alma noticed how her head seemed to look a little different.

'Can I come in?' asked her father.

'Sure!'

Alma closed the drawer and welcomed him into her room.

'You have to keep this open, OK?' her father said, opening her door. 'What can we play with?'

'I don't know.'

'Why don't we go and look in the garden? You might find something you haven't seen before...'

Alma loved surprises.

They went downstairs and out into the garden through the back door.

Parked just in front of it was a beautiful, new, big green bicycle.

'There. You're getting taller now. This one will suit you much better.'

'I love it!' Alma shouted.

'Tomorrow's Saturday, and it's going to be sunny. You can try it on the street then.'

'Yes!' Alma replied, carefully studying every detail of the bike.

Spritz, the cat, was sitting on the garden wall observing the situation, unmoved.

At dinner, Dad talked about his new job and the possibility of living in America.

He seemed to want to convince her mother that it was a good idea to move there and sell the house. Alma didn't even know where America was, exactly; geography wasn't her best subject.

'Does it mean we won't live here any more, Dad?' she asked.

'Yes, but it'll be better. We'll have a bigger house there,' he said.

'We're still talking about it, dear,' her mother concluded. Alma didn't like the sound of all this. But tomorrow she was going to try out her new bicycle. Right now, that was way more important than America.

That night, while Dad read Alma a bedtime story, Almondine patiently waited inside her drawer. *She's becoming very good,* Alma thought.
When the light was out and her father had left, Alma whispered to Almondine about the plans for tomorrow. 'I'm going to take you for a ride on my new bike, Almondine!'

Chapter 19

A Bicycle Ride

It was a beautiful sunny morning.

The bicycle had a nice basket hanging over the handlebars, real lights and even gears. It was a proper, foldable, grown-up's bike.

'Is it still too high, Alma?' her father was checking the seat.

Alma could barely touch the ground with her toes, so her dad had to drop the saddle all the way down.

'It's perfect now, thanks!'

She pushed off slowly, and after a couple of wobbles she found her pace and raced down the pavement to the end of their road.

'Almondine, this is so cool!'

Almondine peeked her little head out of Alma's pocket and looked around.

Alma was gaining more confidence with each lap and began riding faster. They lived on a quiet road, so Alma felt safe.

Her mum recorded the moment on her phone and went back into the house while her father sat next to their front door waiting for Alma to complete her loops down the road. Spritz was also observing the scene from the top of a rubbish bin.

After a few minutes, Alma stopped at the end of the road.

'You can come out, Almondine,' she said while momentarily placing her on the bell. She took off her jacket and squeezed it inside the front basket. Then she gently placed Almondine on top of it. 'Hold on tight, I'm going to take you for a ride!' She pushed off and started pedalling fast. Alma and Almondine both enjoyed speeding along with the warm wind blowing through their hair.

As she approached the house again, Alma saw a car turning into their street. Alma moved towards the side of the road, but hit the mirror of a parked car, which made her wobble. She swerved towards the pavement, pulling on the brakes, but she'd already lost her balance.

She fell off the bike, and landed on the metal grille of a drain.

The car stopped, and a lady rushed out. Alma's mother and father also ran towards her.

Feeling a bit shocked, Alma looked at the palms of her hands, which were grazed. She'd also bruised her knee.

Her father helped her to her feet.

'OK, let's take you inside and get that disinfected,' he said.

'Is she OK?' the lady asked. 'I'm so sorry. I hope it wasn't my fault.'

'I think she's all right, thank you,' Alma's father reassured her. He took Alma's hand and walked to the house with her.

But Alma suddenly remembered Almondine.

'Where is she?!' she shouted.

'Where is who?'

'I need to go back to the bicycle!'

'No, we're going inside now, Alma,' her father said. 'Don't worry about the bicycle. I'm sure it's

fine. I'm going to take care of it.'

Alma pulled away from her father's hand and rushed back to where she'd fallen.

'Almondine! Almondine!' she called, looking in the jacket and around the bicycle.

'Who are you calling?' her father asked as he picked up the bike and rested it against a wall.

Alma was staring down the drain's metal slats.

'Oh, no! Almondine!!'

Chapter 20

Rescue Mission

'Have you dropped something down the drain?' her father said. Her mother had also joined them. 'Almondine, can you hear me?' Alma shouted, ignoring the commotion around her. 'Are you in there? Are you OK?'

A slow gurgling sound came from the drain.

'Oh no… Almondine!!!'

'Mummy,' came a feeble cry, 'I'm here!'

'Oh, Almondine! Stay where you are, I'll find a way to get you out, I promise. Can you hold on where you are?'

Silence.

'Can you hear me?'

'OK. I think so.'

Alma rushed into the house as her father watched, completely bemused.

'Let's go to the bathroom and get you cleaned up,' her mother said, briskly following her.

'Not now, Mum!'

But her mother wasn't going to let her go anywhere until she was done with her.

Those few minutes in the bathroom seemed like an eternity as, in her mind, Alma went through every possible thing that could have happened to Almondine in the drain. Was she in the water? Were there any rats?

Finally, her mother let her go downstairs again. Grabbing a broom, she went back out into the street.

Her father was standing on the pavement in front of their house, straightening the bike's front wheel.

'Careful crossing the

street!' he shouted. 'Where are you going with that broom?'

Spritz was prowling around by the drain.

'Go away!!' Alma scared him off and shouted down the grating.

'Almondine, are you still there?'

'Help, Mummy!'

'Here, grab this! Careful!'

She pushed the broomstick in as far as it would go. It didn't reach the bottom.

'Can you grab it?'

'No.'

'Can you climb up a bit?'

'It's wet. I'm slipping.'

'What, exactly, are you doing with that broom?' came her father's voice. He was standing right next to her.

'Dad, I need a rope! Quick!'

'A rope?'

'Quick, Dad! Now!!!'

'OK, OK… I'll see what I can find.'

He walked off. Alma hoped he'd be quick.

'Almondine, stay there, keep talking to me and stay away from the water.'

After a couple of minutes her father came back with a ball of garden twine.

'Is this OK?'

'Perfect.'

Alma made a knot in the end of the string and dropped it into the drain.

'Tell me when you can reach it!'

Alma dropped the string deeper and deeper into the darkness of the drain.

'I've got it!' Almondine called at last.
Alma could feel the little girl's weight as she pulled down on it.
'Great. Now, hold on tight.'
She raised the string slowly until it had nearly reached the top.
Then she noticed that both Spritz and her father were watching, curious to see what Alma was going to pull out.

Chapter 21

Almondine's Bump

'Don't look!'

Neither of them moved an inch.

'I want to see what you've got in there,' her father said annoyingly.

'I said don't look!!!' Alma had never shown so much determination.

The cat backed off. After a moment, her father sighed and in order to quickly resolve the situation, he obediently turned his back. After all, the mystery of the drain could be solved later.

Alma pulled Almondine out, put her in her pocket and ran into the house.

Her father was left to collect the broom and the loose string.

That evening, Dad was looking forward to spending some time with Alma and finding out all about the drain incident, but Alma insisted she wanted to be alone and closed herself in her room. He didn't like her door being closed again – it was weird for a girl of her age. But since it was late he felt it was best to let her be.

Alma sat on her bed and read Almondine a few pages of her illustrated book of Little Nemo in Slumberland. Almondine immersed herself in those amazing pictures and after a while she fell asleep, with her head full of surreal stories and colourful images.

Alma looked at the cute, innocent little creature and thought about the adventures they'd had together. She felt lucky to have found such a unique little friend, and wanted Almondine to stay with her forever. She made life so much fun, and helped her see everything in a different way. Alma enjoyed watching her discover the world so much that she forgot about the scary moments that came with it.

She felt special, because she was the only one who had found Almondine.

As she lovingly stroked Almondine's hair, she felt something strange. There was definitely a bump on her head. She had already noticed that her head looked different some time ago.

Alma touched the bump gently. What was it? She hoped it was nothing serious. Maybe she had banged her head earlier when she fell?

She gently placed Almondine in the drawer, closed it and went to sleep.

Chapter 22

Fashion Show

Alma's father didn't stay very long. After a few days, he left again for work.

It was sad when Dad wasn't around. The house felt a bit empty, and her mother argued with her more often.

At the same time, it made it easier to play with Almondine. She had more time to herself, and to let her wander around and play in her room.

Alma decided that she wasn't going to take her outside again. It had proven to be too dangerous. And that big bump on her head was so weird. It had seriously begun to worry her, because she

couldn't figure what had caused it. It didn't seem to bother her, but it was still getting longer and bigger.

Aside from the bump, though, Almondine was becoming really beautiful.

She was a bit quieter than she used to be, and although she was still affectionate and playful with Alma, she seemed more mature and sensible.

'Well,' thought Alma, 'my Almondine is growing up.'

The little girl now knew when to hide and when she could roam freely in the room. Alma didn't have to trap her in the drawer any more. She could just tell her to hide when needed. It was all getting a lot easier. Lately, when Alma came back from school, she often found Almondine on the window ledge, leaning against the glass and staring outside. She seemed to be longing for something.

One Saturday morning, when she was still asleep, Alma felt Almondine's hands nudge her cheek.

'Almondine? What's up?'
Alma asked in the darkness.
'Look.'
Alma rubbed her eyes to wake
herself up and got up to draw
the curtain.
It was a beautiful, clear day.
Alma looked at
Almondine.
She was standing on her
bed, smiling. The big bump
on her head had burst into a
gorgeous white flower.
'Do you like it?' Almondine
asked her.
Alma kneeled in front of
Almondine. The flower was
definitely growing out of her head.
It was a bit freaky, but what a magnificent display!
Alma loved it so much she was almost speechless.
'Almondine, you look so pretty.'
The flower had a vivid pink centre and tiny
filaments leading to bright yellow anthers.
'So that's what the bulge was. You had the bud of
a flower on your head!'
Almondine twirled, elegantly waving her head

and arms like a ballerina.

'I like it,' Almondine declared with pride.

'Almondine, you are gorgeous. We can have a fashion show!'

Alma remembered that her dad had given her an instant camera; a chunky plastic toy that ejected little photos soon after taking them.

'I can prepare a red carpet, pick the best costumes, and you can try them all on!'

Alma had lots of choices for Almondine. Some of the dresses were borrowed from her smaller dolls, others were adapted ones from her bigger ones, and still others she made herself with paper cutouts or spare pieces of cloth.

Alma refused to leave the house that day, and Mum had to cancel Alma's invitation to the birthday party of one of her friends.

Mum still insisted that Alma's door had to stay open, so Alma decided to build a tent with a bedsheet, in which she could hide. She was able to play with Almondine all weekend and not be seen. By Sunday evening Alma had used up all the photos in her camera.

Mum told her the tent had to be put away for the

rest of the week, so Alma dismantled everything. But she had already proudly collected all twenty-four instant photos in an envelope.

That night they sat in bed and looked at all the pictures, commenting on each one and trying to decide which was their favourite.

Alma hid the photos at the bottom of the drawer, where her mother was unlikely to look, and they went to sleep.

Chapter 23

Almondine's Longing

Almondine's flower didn't last long. The petals fell off a week later, leaving only a little stem.
But little green shoots were now starting to sprout from her head.
Almondine was changing, outside and inside.
After she lost her flower she became quieter, and Alma had the feeling that she was longing for something she couldn't tell her about. Alma was always thinking up ways for them to have fun together in her room, but now Almondine often gazed out the window, looking bored.
'Almondine, why don't you tell me what's wrong?

I'm sure you'll get another flower soon. We just have to be patient.'
Almondine would just look down sadly, without saying a word. Although Alma guessed that her little friend was simply getting bored of staying inside the room all the time, she was too afraid of allowing her out of the house again. And yet she really felt for her. She couldn't stand seeing her friend unhappy any more, so one day she gave in.

'You want to go out again, don't you?' Alma asked.
Almondine sighed.
'What if we go in the garden tomorrow? Just you and me. I'll make sure you are safe this time.'
Almondine smiled and her eyes lit up with hope.
'We could play in my playhouse,' Alma said, 'and make some slime together.'
Almondine frowned at this.
'Or you could help me plant pansies in little pots, and then we'll put them around the house. Or how about we pick the wild strawberries at the back of the garden? What about that?'

'I'd love that,' Almondine replied.

Alma was very pleased to hear her voice again.

'Great, let's do that; but remember the rules, you have to be careful,' Alma said. 'Well, I guess I have to be careful with you. We've got to stay together all the time, OK?'

The next afternoon was bright and sunny.

Alma walked into the garden, holding her jam jar very carefully. The lid was screwed on, and inside it stood Almondine.

At the back of her garden there was a big patch of wild strawberries.

Her Grandma had planted some when she came to visit two years earlier and they'd spread like weeds over a big area of their lawn, forming a lush bedding of leaves, white flowers and, hidden among them, so many tiny, red, juicy gems, begging to be picked.

Spritz, who was dozing in a grassy spot near a cherry tree, lazily raised his head to watch Alma as she looked for the best spot.

She put the jar down among the leaves and started to pick the ripest strawberries.

Almondine was leaning against the jar, staring out in amazement at the surroundings. To her it looked like a beautiful forest.

Each time Alma's hand was full, she opened the jar and dropped the strawberries inside with Almondine. They smelled beautiful.

Almondine looked up at Alma, hoping to be taken out and allowed to help.

'Almondine, don't look at me like that,' Alma said, 'it's safer for you to stay in there.'

Meanwhile, Spritz found all this too interesting to ignore. He got up and headed over towards them, behind Alma's back.

Getting closer, he noticed a little creature moving inside the jar and his predatory instinct kicked in. He started to slink towards her.

Chapter 24

Wild Strawberries

Alma turned and noticed the cat.

'Get away, you!' Alma said sharply, which was all the signal Spritz needed to back off.

Alma placed the last strawberries inside the jar with Almondine, closed the lid and walked over to her playhouse.

She closed the door behind her and sat at her table with the pots of forgotten slime experiments from last year. She opened Almondine's jar and let her out, then put all the strawberries she'd collected on a plate.

Her table was only one of two shelves, screwed on

to the wall of the little house. Alma needed to clear some space, so she pushed some of the old clutter to one side.

'Let me see… I need to find a bowl and fill it with water, so we can clean the strawberries. What about you, are you thirsty?'

Almondine pointed to a plastic bottle.

'Argh!' Alma shouted suddenly, pushing herself back from the table.

A big, grey spider had crawled out from behind the bottle and was creeping towards her little Almondine.

'Go away!' Alma

ordered the spider, squeamishly. 'Almondine, get back inside the jar!'

But Almondine wasn't frightened at all. She walked towards the spider, stood in front of it and studied it closely.

The spider stopped. Almondine squatted and extended her arm like you do with a puppy. The spider began crawling again towards her hand, then up her arm until it settled on her shoulder.

'That's really freaking me out, Almondine! Aren't you scared?'

Almondine stood up. The spider was feeling her head with its front legs.

'It tickles.'

'I'm sure it does!'

'Why don't you go and fetch the water?' Almondine said. 'We'll wait for you here.'

'Almondine, please get rid of that spider!'

'OK. If she scares you so much, I'll tell her to go.'

'Her?'

'She's a mum.'

'A mum? Whatever… I'm going. Get rid of it… her… OK?'

Alma ran out of the playhouse and into the kitchen, where she asked her mother to give her some water.

When Alma came back into the playhouse with a
pan full of water, she froze with panic.
'Almondine! Where are you?'

Chapter 25

Almondine's New Home

'Mummy, I'm here.'
Almondine was standing on the second shelf.
'She showed me her egg sac. And look, over there!'
Almondine walked across the shelf and pointed to an empty chrysalis.
'A butterfly came out of this! And, you see that knothole in the wall? That's where everyone goes in and out.'
'I'm not sure if I like that,' Alma said. 'We must close it.'
'No, we must not. And look over there, just under the roof.'

Alma looked up, and saw a couple of moths perched upside down.

'Aren't they gorgeous?' Almondine said.

'Mum told me she'd cleaned this place,' Alma replied.

'She did, and the spider mother wasn't too happy about that. Your mum broke all her webs.'

Alma was still rigidly holding the water and staring at Almondine nimbly finding her way back to the table.

'It's OK, Mummy. Sit down. You can put the water here.'

Alma put the pan on the table, and Almondine

undressed and jumped into it.

'Throw the strawberries in,' Almondine said. 'Let's play!'

Alma poured the strawberries into the water, and Almondine played with them like beach balls.

Alma was pleased to see her happy again.

'Why don't you eat them? They're clean now!' Almondine suggested.

So Alma ate the strawberries one by one, and it wasn't long before they were all gone.

Alma looked at the inside of the playhouse, feeling so much more aware of what went on inside it than she'd ever been before.

'I'm getting hungry, too, Mum. Can you get me some soil please?' asked Almondine.

'Of course.'

Alma picked up a small plastic jug and filled it with soft earth from outside the house. Almondine climbed out of the water, shook herself dry, put her dress back on and started eating with both hands.

'This is nice! Much better than the soil from the house plant!'

When Almondine was full, Alma decided that was enough for today.

'Let's go back inside now.'

'No, please, let's not.'

'We can come back tomorrow if you want, Almondine.'

'But I want to stay here.'

'What do you mean?' Alma asked. 'Do you want to sleep here?'

'Yes, why not? It'll be my home, and you can see me whenever you want. I will rearrange these pots and, look, I can use this wooden spoon as a bed...'

'But it could be dangerous at night, Almondine.'

'No, it won't. Nobody will want to hurt me here. I'll be fine.'

They argued about it for a while. Eventually Alma had enough; she grabbed Almondine, put her in the jar and took her back inside the house.

It didn't go well. Almondine took offence. She didn't want to talk to Alma, or even look at her any more. She kept this up for the rest of the evening, and cried all night long.

When Alma woke up, Almondine was still sobbing inside the drawer, where she had been placed for the night.

Alma's heart sank. She couldn't bear it any more. She took Almondine back to the garden and left her in the playhouse.

'See you later,' she said.

Almondine gratefully waved her goodbye.

Alma went to school feeling a bit sad, but hoping for the best.

Chapter 26

Almondine is Gone

Almondine lived in the playhouse from then on. It was better for Alma that she didn't have to struggle to keep Almondine hidden all the time. And now that Alma had stopped shutting her bedroom door, her mother seemed happier and didn't ask awkward questions.

Alma thought it would be like this from now on.

But something happened on the first day of her summer holiday.

It was a lovely Saturday morning, and Alma woke up bubbling with excitement. Their flight to

Spain was booked for the late afternoon, and she had everything prepared for the trip.

Her mother was making sure that the house was in good order, watering the plants and arranging everything so that it could be safely left for the whole month they were going to be away.

Alma had packed a shoebox with a plastic vial filled with water and another with fresh soil, along with her jewellery box, all wrapped up in a soft cloth. The jewellery box seemed comfortable enough for Almondine to hide in during the journey and, importantly, it would avoid any complications at airport security.

She got dressed and finally went to the garden to collect her Almondine.

Spritz was sitting on top of her playhouse, looking down at the door.

Alma shushed him away and went inside. 'Almondine? It's time to go,' she called. 'Almondine! Where are you hiding?'

Almondine usually greeted Alma as soon as she saw her, but this time there was no reply.

'Almondine? Come on, we have to leave today. This isn't the time to play.'

Alma called her again and again.

The sky had become heavy with dense, dark clouds, and thunder had started to rumble in the near distance.

Alma searched the playhouse, inspecting every nook and cranny until a heavy rain started to fall. Alma braved the weather until she was soaking wet, but when her mum saw her, she had to rush back to the house. She got changed and then stared out of her window at the rain and wind battering the garden, feeling terribly worried. Alma didn't want to leave any more but she had no other choice. What on earth could have happened to Almondine?

When they left Alma cried.

Chapter 27

Alma's Birthday

It was Alma's saddest summer holiday.

You might not think it was so bad. After all, she spent four weeks swimming in the sea, having picnics with her Grandma and her cousins, slurping ice-creams, playing with Rex and jumping on the trampoline every day – which was her favourite pastime.

But none of it stopped her from feeling sad, especially in the evenings when she remained alone in her bed.

Her ninth birthday was due on the last week of the holiday. She usually loved her birthdays in Spain, but this time she really didn't enjoy it.

She missed Almondine so much.

And as if that wasn't enough, her mother told her that her father had accepted the new job in America. The house had already been sold, and they would be preparing to leave as soon as they got back to London.

It seemed her life was going to change a lot.

Would she ever see Almondine again? She wished she could be with her little friend again, the way they used to be.

Alma often looked at Grandad's almond tree. After all, that was where Almondine had come from. Was it a magic tree? Were more Almondines growing on it? She'd already checked and shaken all the newly picked almonds in their green hulls. None of them made a sound.

One evening, Grandad asked Alma to help him pick the last few almonds left on the tree.

She was holding the same pretty little basket she'd found Almondine in, only nine months earlier.

'Have you ever eaten them green?' Grandad asked, up on his short ladder.

'No. I don't want to eat them.'

Alma carefully shook and listened to each nut that he dropped before placing it in the basket.

'Why are you shaking them?' chuckled Grandad.

'Have you ever found anything unusual in these almonds?' asked Alma.

'They all seem the same to me, but sometimes you do find one that's better than the others.'

Alma was intrigued by his answer.

'What do you mean?'

'When your mother was your age, she used to say that some almonds were better than others.'

'Mum? What did she mean by better?'

'I don't know. They all taste the same to me.'

Moments later, Alma grabbed hold of her mother and questioned her very seriously.

'Mum, did you ever find a special almond?'

'In what way?'

'Well...' Alma hesitated, still unsure whether she should reveal her secret. 'One that's alive.'

Her mother smiled.

'When I was a child, we didn't have many toys. I could bring anything to life. We made little dollies out of poppy stalks, or drew faces on acorns and painted their hoods like hats…'

'But what about the almonds? Did you ever find a real little girl inside one of them?' Alma finally pleaded.

'A girl in an almond?' Mum asked back with a loving smile.

'Mum, I'm serious.'

'Yes. Why not? Could have happened. I don't really remember. But I suppose I might have.'

Alma thought her mother wasn't really properly listening to what she was saying.

You couldn't forget finding a real baby inside an almond! Alma thought. *And if she did, why on earth wouldn't she tell me? Mum believes once again I'm just imagining things.*

She concluded it hadn't happened to her. She asked her Grandma too and her question simply made her laugh.

Alma became convinced that Almondine was indeed unique, and it made her even sadder to have lost her.

And she still didn't know exactly who or what she was, how she came to be, or where in the world she'd gone now.

Chapter 28

Alma Leaves

Alma and her parents spent their first two weeks back in London packing all their belongings into sturdy cardboard boxes of all shapes and sizes.

It was quite incredible how many boxes they needed, especially for Alma's books, toys, games and dolls.

As Alma sifted through her stuff, a lot of things reminded her of Almondine: the photos of her walking on the red carpet, for instance, and looking so pretty. She could be mistaken for a little doll. Who would have guessed that she was real, that she could talk, and that she'd lived with Alma for nine whole months?

Every evening Alma went out to look around the garden again.

Deep down, she was still hoping to find Almondine. She couldn't accept that her little friend would abandon her or, worse, that she might be dead.

Spritz sometimes strolled across the overgrown lawn, but it seemed that even he didn't bother greeting Alma any more.

Soon came the day when a big van parked in front of their house, and two strong men took away all the piled-up boxes. It was weird to see their home so bare.

For three days, they stayed with a neighbour while they completed the last few chores before their long journey.

When the time to leave came, they returned into their old empty home for one last time. While they were waiting for their taxi, something very unexpected happened.

Alma was sitting in her empty room and sifting through Almondine's old photos, when she heard a tap on the window.

A wood pigeon was staring into the room.

Alma got up and lifted the sash window. Seeing Alma, it took off.

And there, on the sill, was Almondine.

She wasn't wearing her dress, and her body was covered in green leaves. But Alma could still see her cute little face.

She smiled at Alma and opened her arms, which now looked more like twigs. Alma picked her up, then put out a finger, which Almondine hugged fondly. She had grown so much. Alma asked her lots of questions: how she'd disappeared, if she was well, what she'd been doing all this time, and if she'd been treated kindly by the other creatures she'd met.

Almondine patiently explained everything that had happened to her over those mysterious last few weeks, and Alma listened keenly to the whole story.

She had survived an incredible journey, and Alma could hardly believe all that had happened to her. She was so glad Almondine was alive and safe now.

She looked for a place to hide her but Almondine immediately insisted on being left in their old garden. Alma couldn't understand why she would not follow her, but Almondine seemed to have changed beyond her appearance. Her heart had changed too. She was ready for a new life. Then her mother called from downstairs. It was time to go. Alma begged her, but there was nothing she could say or do to make her tiny friend change her mind. Finally, Almondine gave Alma's finger a long, warm hug and asked to be placed back on the window ledge. Almost immediately, the wood pigeon landed next to her again. She climbed on its back, and that was it. They waved goodbye one last time and she was gone.

Alma wiped away a little tear, but then she smiled. After all, if Almondine was going to be happy, so was she.

Her mum called her again and she went downstairs. Their taxi was waiting for them and so was her new life in America.

Epilogue

This book isn't long enough to tell you about all the things that happened to Almondine in the summer, after Alma left.

The teeny-weeny girl endured an extraordinary adventure out on her own, while she grew up; one that deserved to be recorded in a diary.

I hope you'll also find someone like Almondine to play with and care for. And even if you don't find a girl inside an almond, magic can be everywhere. Just stay curious and open.

Your most special discovery is waiting for you where you least expect it.

Almondine's Cupcakes

Here is a weird cupcake Alma made for Almondine.
Though she really loved it, you will definitely want to swap these weird ingredients to bake one you can actually eat and enjoy!

a)   2 cups of good quality compost

b)   1/4 cup of fine wood chips

c)   1/4 teaspoon of worms casts

d)   1/2 teaspoon of crushed dried leaves

e)   1/4 cup of smashed banana peel

f)   6 drops of squeezed used teabags.

g)   2 finely ground eggshells

h)   1 teaspoon of rose or other flower petals

i)   3 tablespoons of rainwater

For a human-friendly, tasty Chocolate Cupcake, simply swap with these ingredients in the same measure:

a) Coconut flour; b) Cocoa; c) Salt; d) Baking Soda; e) Coconut Oil; f) Liquid Stevia; g) Eggs; h) Vanilla Extract; i) Hot water.

You need to ask for a grown-up's supervision before mixing and baking these cakes!

Instead, for a Smoothy Slime ONLY fit for an Alien, swap with these ingredients in the same measure:

a) Shaving foam; b) PVA Glue; c) Food colouring; d) Glitter; e) Transparent PVA glue; f) Perfume; g) A pinch of bicarbonate of soda; h) Contact lens solution; i) Foam balls.

Once again, remember to ask for a grown-up's supervision!

Please write a review

Please let Gabriele Zucchelli know what you thought about *Almondine* by leaving your review on the online store where you bought this book.

If you are under age 13 please ask a grown up to help you.

Discover more!

For more information, bonus material, activities and other curiosities, please visit **almondine.club**

Social Media

The Author is aware of some of the concerns surrounding the potentially addictive use of social media and is not an advocate of such platforms in general for children.
If you are the parent and if you are happy to contribute to the books' visibility with a Comment or 'Like', you can find the links on:
almondine.club

Thank you!

About the Author

Gabriele grew up in Italy where he discovered the awesome art of animation when he was only twelve years old.
Some years later in Milan, he met some very talented animators, who became his first teachers. He hasn't stopped animating and working in this field ever since.

He's worked on a lot of well-known films ever since moving to London, firstly using pencil and paper, and later with computers. More than twenty-five years have now passed since his first job in the UK – the animated version of *Peter Rabbit and Friends* – and the more recent ones – *The Jungle Book* and *The Lion King*.
A few years ago he also directed a historical documentary on the first ever animated feature films: *Quirino Cristiani*.

The *Almondine* trilogy is his first work as an author of children's books.

Are you wondering what happened to Almondine when she disappeared from Alma's garden? And then after that? Find out in the next books:

ALMONDINE GROWS UP
Book 2

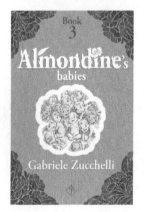

ALMONDINE'S BABIES
Book 3

My Thoughts and Drawings

Would you like to share your thoughts and pictures?

Take a snapshot and ask a grown-up to share it on the blog at:

almondine.club

Cut your Bookmark!

Book 1

Almondine

Printed in Great Britain
by Amazon

63157666R00112